DESTINY

Date
2/11/08

Presented to
John

by
Medea Chitauro
@hitauro

Thanx John 4
everything
and i believe

God's gonna
raise u
up to
new
heights

DESTINY

Medea Chitauro

PNEUMA SPRINGS PUBLISHING UK

First Published 2008
Published by Pneuma Springs Publishing

Destiny
Copyright © 2008   Medea Chitauro
ISBN: 978-1-905809-31-8

Cover design, editing and typesetting by:
Pneuma Springs Publishing

A Subsidiary of Pneuma Springs Ltd.
7 Groveherst Road, Dartford Kent, DA1 5JD.
E: admin@pneumasprings.co.uk
W: www.pneumasprings.co.uk

A catalogue record for this book is available from the British Library.

ACKNOWLEDGMENTS

There are a number of people who contributed to my becoming a published author. Above all I would like to say a big thank you to God for making the whole publishing experience happen. I want to thank my family especially my mother for her support and being my best friend. My gratitude goes to Nadah Matambanadzo who believed in me from the beginning and encouraged me to go for my dream. Also thanks to Getrude Musiiwa for her enthusiasm and encouragement. Finally thanks to my publisher who made my publishing dream a reality.

One

Mel Donovan woke up panicking. She felt like the walls were closing in on her in the house she lived with her parents. It was a luxurious property in a plush highly sought after location in North London. It consisted of a lounge, dining room, TV room, kitchen or breakfast room, four double bedrooms, garden with patio area and double garage. It was over a year since she broke up with Brandon but her heart was still broken. Almost every night she was woken up by the recurring nightmare of when they separated. Mel remembered vividly how it happened. It was a glorious summers day; the sun was shining in a cloudless sky and they where going balling and strolling in the park. Mel's eyes sparkled when she greeted him at the doorstep. He was very good-looking, tall, and slim and had a very sturdy face with striking features. He was dark in complexion unlike Mel and had the most amazing brown eyes. The main reason Mel loved him so much was how he made her feel; she felt so special whenever they were together. He made her feel like she was the most beautiful girl, he was also very attentive and caring. All in all he was her dream guy and everyday she thanked God for him. They had been going out for over a year but every time they met it was still magical like when she had first laid eyes on him. When they were together she felt very happy and missed him terribly when they were apart. They had never had any major arguments and whenever he upset her he would bring a box of chocolates and flowers. He was so adorable and it was always so easy to forgive him.

"Ready for our date," he had said cheerfully looking at her closely "you look smashing as usual."

Mel had surely dressed to impress and was wearing a wide strap v-neck blue dress in patch dyed cotton fabric which had a semi low back with a pair of blue sandals. She was tall and slim and knew what clothes complimented her figure the most. She was a beautiful black girl who was outgoing and had delicate features on a beautiful face. Her hair which was dark and thick was usually tied in a pony tail and this emphasised her stunning facial features even more. The most amazing thing about her was her character. She was friendly, caring and generally a warm person to be around.

"Thanks! You do not look so bad yourself," Mel said full of smiles.

"Don't be shy to say how fine I look," he said smugly. He was dressed in baggy jeans, T-shirt and Nike trainers.

"You always look great so I've run out of compliments," she said truthfully.

"Anyway let's not waste time because of my curfew. Remember my parents want me back home before 10 P.M."

"I don't think a nineteen year old should have a curfew," his voice showed disapproval.

"You are over eighteen."

"I know, but my parents are strict and as long as I live under their roof I will have to obey their rules. I know they mean well. Remember the bible commands us to honour our parents," she said with emphasis. Mel was a devoted Christian as well as her family and tried her best to please God.

"Here we go again with you preaching," he said teasing but something about his facial expressions showed he was annoyed by her constant reference of the bible. He was a Christian himself but didn't seem as devoted as she was.

"We better bounce then," she said walking towards the car. The last thing she wanted was to build tension between them because of the news she wanted to share with him later that day. Their date went on well as usual and they enjoyed each other's company. Mel found it difficult to find the right moment to communicate what had been on her mind for a while. When he was driving her home she still hadn't told him even though she knew she had to tell him sooner rather than later.

"I'm pregnant," she blurted out without warning.

"What!" Brandon screamed and almost lost control of the wheel.

"I'm pregnant", she repeated more quietly this time shocked by Brandon's response. She was expecting a strong reaction but the way his face changed from being soft to hard scared her. He seemed like a totally different person; his jaw tightened when he spoke again.

"So what are you going to do about it?"

"What do you mean by that?" She was beginning to get angry too and rather frustrated.

"I will have the baby of course, because the bible teaches against abortion," she said.

"And the bible says you should become pregnant when you are not married," he said coldly in a sarcastic way.

"How dare you say that," she found herself yelling "don't

make it seem like it's entirely my fault. It takes two you know, I never wanted to sleep with you but you were very persuasive and told me you loved me and wanted to spend the rest of your life with me."

"I didn't mean it," he said without even flinching. Mel couldn't believe what she was hearing. Looking into his eyes there was no compassion and no hint of remorse. It was as if he was someone else. He had never showed this side of him before and Mel could have sworn that he wasn't capable of behaving in such a malicious way. She hadn't told her parents she was pregnant and knew they wouldn't be pleased at all as they thought she was still a virgin.

"No need to start arguing. If you need time to digest this I understand," she said quivering but trying her best to remain calm.

Brandon looked at Mel and said tonelessly "There is nothing to think about. All I know is I don't want to see you again, I don't want anything to do with you anymore." Mel couldn't accept what she was hearing. She thought he was joking but the look in his eyes told her he was dead serious. This was the last time he had spoken to her. Even though she had seen him at university campus before she dropped out, he had totally ignored her.

Mel sat up in bed and looked at the bedside clock. It's only 5.30am, and I've been awake for well over an hour she thought. She felt so alone, she had recently had a miscarriage and the nightmare of when the doctors told her the baby had died was unbearable. She never stopped blaming herself as the doctors had said her depression and stress during the pregnancy could have contributed to the miscarriage.

"My baby," she whispered in the dark. She hadn't bothered to switch on the light.

"Brandon, how could you leave me like that?" Somehow she thought if they had been together she would have been able to cope better. Ever since their split her life had become unbearable. When she told her parents she was pregnant they showed disapproval but nevertheless showed her unconditional love. She was ashamed to go to church and it didn't help when some people didn't particularly want to associate with her anymore. Mel felt she had disgraced her family and let down her parents who were church leaders. She felt very guilty about what she did with Brandon and was finding it hard to pray to God. She was bleeding inside and all she wanted was someone to give her a hug and tell her she didn't have to continue in shame and guilt because God forgives our transgressions and loves us unconditionally. Instead she got judgemental stares and rebuke for her actions and indiscretion. She had beat up her self mentally and had experienced enough pain and just wanted someone to tell her how she could turn away from her past and move forward with life. She felt very unworthy to be in God's presence and asking him for anything was certainly not something Mel felt privileged to do. Up until that time, whenever she had a need she would simply pray and praise God for the answer, or she would fast and pray if she felt she needed to do so, but now the story was different; she had stopped praying because she felt so unworthy. Mel kept going to church to please her parents but her heart had become ice cold, she was no longer moved by the worship or the messages, she was only going through the motions.

Another Sunday had come round again and Mel was not particularly looking forward to going to church as usual. It's only around five, Mel thought with despair. She knew falling asleep again was going to be difficult and started contemplating what she could do. Reading the bible crossed her mind but she dismissed the thought. She couldn't remember the last time she read the bible on her own. Mel continued to lay in bed thinking about giving up on herself.

She didn't know how long she could continue to go on feeling the way she felt, she felt there was no one to turn to. On the outside she was putting on a brave face smiling, and acting as if all was well but only God knew how she was really feeling. Mel was the type of person who didn't like to burden or worry others therefore she kept her feelings from her parents. She had a younger brother aged sixteen but she couldn't possibly speak to him about her problems.

"Mel, Mel," she was woken up again by the sound of her mother's voice calling her. When she looked at the clock again it was 9.15am. Church was starting at 10 o'clock and she had overslept. She must have fallen asleep again without warning. She quickly got out of bed and went straight to the bathroom to have a shower. Within minutes she had finished washing and dressing and rushed downstairs to join her family.

"Good morning Mum, Dad and Joe," she greeted them and sat down to join them for breakfast. They all seemed so happy and Mel was struggling to keep on a happy face.

"You alright darling?" Her mother asked concerned. She wasn't fooled by Mel trying to keep up appearances.

"I'm fine", she lied.

"I've been praying that God will give you the strength to deal with the miscarriage. I know it's been five months and I can't imagine how you must be feeling."

"I am alright Mum"; Mel said fighting back the tears

"A pastor from Zimbabwe is preaching today. I have a feeling there is going to be a divine move of God today," her father predicted. Mel was not bothered. No one can help me, not even God, she thought.

"We better get going," her mother stood up to clear the table and Mel helped.

"We don't want to be late"

They rushed to the family car; a Jaguar and managed to arrive at church on time.

When the preacher from Zimbabwe came on the pulpit he started singing a song that touched the hearts of the people.

"You don't have to worry, and don't be afraid, joy comes in the morning. There is a friend in Jesus who will wipe away your tears; say to Jesus my life is in your hands. If your heart is broken, say I know that I can make it, I know that I can stand no matter what may come my way, my life is in your hands."

As people sang this song Mel started crying. She didn't know why she was crying exactly but it was like her spirit was crying out. She started praying in tongues which she had never done before. The other church members joined her in prayer and without notice people were speaking in tongues and praising God. The pastor that day preached about God's mercy. He read a few verses which touched Mel. John 10 verse 10 which says "the thief does not come unless it is to steal and slay and destroy. I have come that they might have life and might have it in abundance." He explained that God wants us to prosper, have peace and wants the best for us in life but the devil wants to destroy our happiness and cause chaos and strife in our lives. He re- confirmed this by reading Jeremiah 29 verse 11-12 which says "for I know the thoughts that I think toward you, saith the Lord, thoughts of peace, and not of evil, to give you an expected end." He said that God loves us so much that he was wounded for our transgressions, bruised for our iniquities and the chastisement of our peace was upon him (Isaiah 53 verse 5). He explained that this means that Jesus has already suffered for us so we don't have to suffer anymore and if we confess our transgressions he is ready to forgive us. He preached that the devil tries to convince us that our circumstances and situations, weaknesses and personality will never change;

13

but the devil is a liar because all these things can be changed through the love of God and we have authority to change our circumstances.

When the pastor was preaching Mel felt something changing inside her. It was as if he was speaking directly to her; she was absorbing every word into her heart. He announced an altar call and began singing 'you don't have to worry' again and started calling for those who were heavy laden, heart broken and those who felt far from God to come forward. He said that when Jesus came on earth he came for those people and sometimes in churches these people's needs are not met.

Mel rushed to the altar not even thinking about who was watching. She knew there were people in church who were there to observe who was been prayed for but all that didn't matter. She was tired of hurting and just wanted to be set free. When it was her turn to be prayed for the pastor gave her a hug and whispered in her ear that he felt that was what she needed. He prophesied that God was going to use her greatly and the devil had been trying to destroy her because he knew the plans God has for her. He said that God was going to heal her broken heart and all things the devil had stolen would be restored; her joy and peace was going to be multiplied. He stated that God is able to do exceedingly, abundantly and above all we could ever ask or think and is able to handle anything that concerns us. For the first time Mel felt someone cared about her situation and was not judging her. She started sobbing when she realized that even though she had been avoiding God he was loving enough to show her mercy and let her know he cared for her always.

"You need to take time to pray and fast in order to break strongholds," he said letting her go.

"Your best days are not behind you but ahead of you sister." Mel felt relieved as if a heavy weight has been lifted from her. I can pray now, she thought excitedly. Just being able to pray gave her huge thrills. She knew that the enemy had been hindering her from praying because blessings and peace from God were released by prayer and praises.

Two

"*W*ere you blessed today?" her mother asked as they ate their dinner of stewed shin of beef with mushroom dumplings that Mrs Donovan had prepared. She was a great cook and had taught Mel to cook from an early age. She saw for the first time in months real joy from Mel. "I was extremely blessed today," Mel replied smiling, "I feel like a heavy burden has been lifted from my life. I feel so free and my heart is rejoicing."

"Praise God for that. I have been praying to God to set you free because when he does you will be free indeed. He will give you peace and joy even in the midst of trouble," Mrs Donovan said full of confidence. Mel kept quiet for a moment contemplating what her mother had just told her and then tearfully said "I know I have been going to church all my life but I was far from God. Now I understand that God is full of love and mercy and he has good thoughts towards me." Mrs Donovan was stunned by Mel's boldness when she talked about God. She had heard Mel speaking about the word of God before but not with such faith. "I know honey; God can just transform your life in an instance. Just one encounter with God and your life will never be the same again." Mrs Donovan paused as she remembered when she first encountered God and thought it would be a good idea to share it with Mel again. "You know like I have told you before, my family were not Christians and my life was a mess. I spent most of my time in the streets, getting drunk and hanging out with the wrong crowd. I used to cause havoc for my parents; shoplifting, stealing from them and not coming back home for days. All in all I would say that I was a nightmare and if it wasn't for God I would have ended up dead or in jail."

"It's hard to believe you did all those things. You are the nicest, loving and most honest person I know. How did you become a Christian then?" Mel asked curiously. She had heard the story before but had never really paid too much attention to remember every detail.

"One day I went home with a man I had just met from the club. The man beat me up really badly to the extent that my face was disfigured and I could hardly walk. He threw me out in the street; I didn't know where I was and I had no money. A woman came to me when she found me crying and shivering in the street. That woman showed me so much compassion and gave me about a hundred pounds to go home with a taxi and sort myself out. She gave me the name of her church and address and said I should come one day".

Mrs Donovan stopped speaking and took a bite into her dumplings. They had been talking for some time now and their food had gone cold. Mel realised her food was cold too but she didn't care. She was so intrigued by her mother's story that food was the last thing on her mind. Mel decided she would reheat her food later. Her father and brother had finished eating their food way before they started their conversation as they were rushing to watch a football match in the TV room.

"Mum please continue with your story," Mel pleaded pushing her plate aside on the table. Mrs Donovan continued to tell Mel how after a few weeks she still thought about that woman who had helped her. She felt compelled to go and thank her properly so went to the church. That day she said the pastor preached about how people who do evil will go to hell and how if we repent God will forgive your sins and talked about the benefits of giving your life to Jesus which includes having eternal life. Mrs Donovan told her daughter that she repented and gave her life to Jesus that day. She didn't want to suffer anymore in her life and had faith that having a relationship with God might give her happiness and fill the void in her life.

"I tried to fill that void with a lot of things that did not satisfy me for example boyfriends and nightclubs but Jesus is the only one who could satisfy me," Mrs Donovan said strongly and her words rang out with deep, heartfelt sincerity. She told Mel that from that day her life changed for the better. Even though she faced many trials and tribulation she still held on to her faith and didn't lose heart or lose her mind. She cleaned up her act and went on to get a teaching degree and eventually married a great man of God. Mrs Donovan was a superb teacher, with warmth that made being around her a pleasure. She had an oval face that was interesting and beautiful. She was very light in complexion and had big hazel eyes. She had a shapely figure that made her female students envious. She always dressed smartly but she was unaware of how beautiful she was. The woman who helped her was Mrs Combs, she became her spiritual mother. She was a middle aged woman, with a very pleasant disposition and a heart of gold. She told Mrs Donovan the enemy was trying to wreck her life because he knew of the destiny she had.

"It is important that you read the bible regularly to build your faith as faith comes from hearing and hearing by the word of God. You just need to surrender all your burdens to God for he cares for you. There is nothing too impossible for God and you just need to know that you can do all things through Christ who strengthens you," Mrs Donavan advised her daughter.

"Thanks mum for your prayers. You are truly a great woman of God. I never understood why you are such a devoted Christian but now I understand that if it wasn't for his love and grace you know you wouldn't have so much joy, peace and prosperity like you have right now," Mel said with wisdom leaning back in her chair.

"As long as I live I will continue to preach his goodness and praise him, because of who he is, my Provider, Prince of peace, Everlasting Father and more. He delivered me from evil and shocked everyone who thought I would never amount to anything," Mrs Donovan said.

"I need to be what God called me to be and walk in my destiny. I will continue to build my faith as I remember reading in the bible that without faith it is impossible to please God. My confidence is in the Lord," Mel added excitedly.

"Lets close in prayer," Mrs Donovan proposed, she prayed Philippians 1 verse 6 which says "we will be confident that he who had began a good work in you will be faithful to complete it." They called Joe and Mr Donovan and they all prayed together. It was a ritual in their home; they never went to bed without praying together. They said goodnight to each other and dispersed. Mel was going to be home in the morning as she neither worked nor went to school. Everyone on the other hand was waking up early in the morning so wanted to retreat to bed early. Mrs Donovan kept thanking God in her heart for delivering Mel from a broken heart and depression.

Three

*I*t had been weeks since Mel's transformation and this day her cousin who lived in Birmingham came to visit. She was two years older than Mel and unlike Mel her life was in order. She had a good job and was engaged to a very good man. In the last year Mel had distanced herself from Tanya because she was beginning to be jealous of how perfect her life seemed. She invited Tanya wanting to reconcile their differences. They used to be great friends before. Tanya was short in stature, beautiful, social and intelligent.

"Let's go to the town centre and spend the day there. We will do a bit of shopping, relax and eat out," Mel proposed glancing out of the window. It was a cold and raw afternoon with a south westerly wind driving the temperature well below five degrees. The cold weather is not going to stop me from going out, Mel thought.

"That's cool. Should we get a taxi or you want me to drive?" Tanya asked still sitting on the couch in the lounge.

"We can use your car if you are not tired from driving a long way to London," she replied. Tanya decided it would be better if they take her car so that they could have the flexibility of driving around.

"So what are your plans for the future? What are your goals

and dreams in life?" Tanya asked Mel as they hit the shops. She knew Mel had dropped out of university, wasn't working and didn't have any money and had to rely on her parents for handouts.

"I'm not too sure. I am just trying to get my life back on track," Mel replied and remembered how Tanya was always probing and questioning her about her future plans. That was one of the reasons she cut her off from her life because she was always asking questions about when she was going to sort out her life and stop feeling sorry for herself. This time Mel didn't mind and was happy to have someone who cared enough to tell her that she needed to put her life in order.

"I mean do you have any plans of going back to university or getting a job?"

"I have enquired at university about going back and they said I have to wait until next year to apply as they had already filled places for the September intake. I am going to start looking for a job from next week. I don't want to keep asking my parents for money." Mel's parents had told her they were quite happy to support her until she got back on her feet. Her family were not millionaires but they were well off. Her parents had well paying jobs and could afford to take care of their children's needs and live comfortably.

"Good for you cousin. I know that you can do anything as long as you put your mind to it. Remember to dream big and as you said earlier God will provide and dreams do come true", Tanya encouraged Mel.

"It's true. I have been studying the New Testament and I realised that God needs our faith to work in our life. Whenever Jesus healed someone or performed any miracle most of the time he would say your faith has made you well. It was those people's faith that made them receive healing and more."

*A*fter her cousin had gone Mel started contemplating about her life. She wanted a fresh start for her life so she began to think about where she wanted to be a few years from now. She sat in her room alone writing down what she wanted to achieve. The first thing on her list was to go back to university. Somehow she didn't feel as passionate about being an accountant like she had before. Now she wanted a career which involved helping people in need. A few careers came to her mind and somehow she kept being drawn to psychology. She knew counselling would be something she could do very well and be fulfilling for her. That same day she started looking up universities which offered psychology and ordered application forms. The next thing on her list was to find a job. She sent out her CV to different companies that same day.

When her family arrived in the evening Mel was exhausted. She had done a lot of reading, research and writing. Even though she was exhausted it didn't stop her from preparing dinner. Her mother was pleased to see Mel preparing dinner as normally she would be slumbering in her room.

"How are you mum? How was work?" Mel asked when her mother joined her in the kitchen. She taught business studies at a local college.

"I'm fine and work was good. How was your day?"

"My day was good. Just have been very busy today," Mel answered with a big smile. She told her mother what she had been up to that day and she was impressed. She saw a positive change in Mel everyday and she knew it was God who was responsible.

"I just want to be proactive like Ruth from the bible. From reading her book I learned that hard work opens doors and great women are not lazy and don't look for handouts. Ruth didn't sit around feeling sorry for herself after her husband died but worked very hard in the fields until Boaz noticed her. I am going to work hard in whatever I do and God will bless the work of my hands. Slumbering is a thing of the past for me," Mel said strongly.

"Way to go girl," Mrs Donovan complimented Mel.

"I always believed sooner or later you will turn your life around and thanks for cooking dinner. What are you preparing?" she asked leaning closer to the cooker. Mel was happy to see how proud her mother was of her.

"I'm making braised meatballs with peppers and tomatoes. We will have it with pasta."

"Thanks honey. I appreciate you helping around the house", she said giving Mel a pat on the back. After a while Mrs Donovan excused herself and went to have a shower. She heard her husband speaking to Joe and knew he had finished bathing. After a while Mel had set the table and was calling everyone to come to the dining table to have their dinner. When everyone had sat down she started bringing the food from the kitchen. Her mother offered to help but Mel said she could manage on her own. She wanted her mother to rest after a long day at work.

"I heard from your mum you are looking for universities to study psychology," Mr Donovan said as he ate the meatballs with his salad.

"Know that you have my blessing and if you need any support whether financial or emotional we are here for you". Her father was a very tall muscular man, but was surprisingly very sensitive and caring.

"Thanks Dad. I know I can count on you and mum but this time I don't want to rely on you to bail me out every time, I want to be more independent." Mel said indignantly.

"Fair enough love but know that you don't have to try and make it on your own when we can help."

"I know. I will definitely come to you if I need your help but hopefully it will be more on the emotional side than financially."

Four

Mel managed to get a place to study psychology at Monsoon University which was 100 miles away from home. This meant she would have to stay at the halls of residence at the university. Monsoon University was a dynamic organisation, formed from a diverse range of specialist institutions. Its long history of academic excellence, learning and research was founded on the technical and trade education of the late 18th century. It is one of the largest universities in the UK with over 30,000 students at its centre in Southampton. Mel was offered a place in the comfortable and safe halls of residence at relatively low cost, close to the city campus.

Mel was very interested in studying how people think, act, react and interact which made her sure she had chosen the right profession. Psychology is concerned with all aspects of behaviour and the thoughts, feelings and motivation underlying such behaviour. Mel had plans of moving to counselling psychology when she finished her degree. Counselling psychologists apply psychology to working collaboratively with people managing difficult life events such as bereavement, past and present relationships and working with mental health issues and disorders. Mel knew the battlefield was in the mind and from past experience she knew that if the mind was not well then other aspects of the person's life will be affected. Helping someone achieve a right mindset was a pleasure to Mel. Because she was going to be living far from home Mel was determined to learn to drive so that she could easily travel home during holidays. Before she started university Mel had passed her driving test. It took seven months of intensive driving lessons and dedication for Mel to pass her test. She managed to save three thousand pounds from her job as a receptionist at a local hotel for the car. Her father helped her pay the balance needed for the car because he was impressed at how she managed to save a lot of money in a short period. Unlike in the past, Mel was not spending all her money on clothes and shoes but saving some of her money for future ventures. She bought a fairly new Toyota Yaris as it was her favourite car at the time.

Mel impressed lecturers with her hard work and excellent grades. She kept studying the word of God and shared it with others. She found a local church which she attended every Sunday unless she was at her home in London. She only had one best friend Amanda and the other students shunned her. They perceived Mel as being too uptight and fake. She always declined their offers of going out or drinking alcohol which made them dislike her. Mel didn't care about trying to fit in the crowd if it meant compromising her beliefs. She knew God said His children shouldn't be conformed to the world but be transformed by the renewing of their minds. Mel wasn't uptight or fake but quite friendly and honest but it was only that people didn't understand that there could be people who loved God and righteousness and were also nice and down to earth at the same time. What surprised Mel is that the same people who despised her would come to her when they were in need or for advice. Mel didn't send them away but helped them whole heartedly if she could. She faced a challenge when a girl called Tamara who used to be horrible to her and did her best to poison people's mind against her came knocking at her door crying and looking for comfort. Tamara was in her early twenties, with long blond hair and a clear milky complexion. She was rugged-looking, dressed in tight straight jeans, over sized t-shirt and slippers. Her face was pale and gaunt, and her eyes were red and swollen and her hair was dishevelled. At first Mel was irritated at her but knew that God wanted her to love her enemies and do well to everyone. After a while compassion overwhelmed Mel and she started comforting Tamara. She was upset because she had just been dumped by her boyfriend after she found him in bed with another woman.

Tamara looked at Mel and began to sob uncontrollably.

"How could he do this to me," Tamara said sobbing," I have always showed him love and when I walked in on him with another woman he didn't bother to say sorry but dumped me saying I meant nothing to him and he was lying when he used to tell me he loved me." Mel handed her a box of tissues listening quietly. When she had finished ranting about how she wasn't going to be able to live without him and wished she was dead Mel intervened.

"What makes you think you can't make it without him?" she asked soothingly. Tamara sat in a small chair, stiff and rigid and looked like she was thinking hard and answered,

"because I love him," she moaned.

"I know what it feels like feeling like life is over when you break up with someone you love but believe me life gets better. You are a beautiful girl and you will definitely fall in love again and probably next time it will be with a man who is worthy of your love. This situation will not break you but will only make you stronger and I am talking from experience."

"How can you give me advice on love when your love life is non existent," even in misery Tamara managed to say rudely. Mel was on her final year of a four year degree and yet she had not managed to find that special person all the time she was at university. She had been on a few dates with some potential boyfriends but nothing worked out. She couldn't engage in a relationship with most of them because they didn't share her faith and wanted to sleep with her. Some guys on the other hand wouldn't pursue a relationship with her because she was honest about the type of guy she liked. Someone who loved God, hardworking and believed in sex after marriage. Those who couldn't conform to these requirements ran fast.

"I have been in love before and suffered heartbreak when my boyfriend dumped me. It might also surprise you how much wisdom you can get from God and reading the bible. There is everything you need to know about relationships, marriage and life in general in the bible. You will be amazed."

"Ease off on that bible stuff. I am an atheist. I don't believe in that stuff," Tamara said with a raised voice as if she was offended. Mel didn't give in, she had experience of dealing with the so called atheist and some have even turned to God later.

"It's a shame you don't believe in God but know that he loves you more than you can ever comprehend. He is just waiting for you to turn to him and he will receive you whatever your situation and what you have done and you know what he can easily heal your broken heart."

"Enough of the preaching Mel," Tamara yelled a thoughtful expression on her face.

"I just need to know how I can get back my boyfriend." Mel was shocked. She was surprised that a very beautiful and confident girl who was full of herself like Tamara would want to get back with someone like her boyfriend Tyris after the way he had treated her. Tyris was short and stocky, with a muscular body and a very attractive face. He had sharp blue eyes and usually dressed in sports clothes.

"Why would you want to get back with someone like Tyris? You've just told me he used to beat you and it wasn't the first time he's cheated."

"I love him," Tamara said defiantly.

"I really love him."

"You should love yourself enough not to go out with someone who abuses you both verbally and physically."

"He only did it a few times throughout our three year relationship and I had offended him," Tamara tried to defend him.

Mel suddenly felt drained. "It doesn't matter what you did. A real man shouldn't hit a woman whatever circumstance. He should be protecting you not you needing protection from him. Let me ask you something and you should answer honestly. Is Tyris your dream guy?"

"I guess so. He is very handsome and has a great body and I love him so much," Tamara said dryly. Mel was not convinced. She knew almost every girl has a dream guy and usually composed of more things than what Tamara had just said.

"Do you mean your dream guy is someone with a great body and handsome face? I know a dream is usually hard to find and yours is not hard because there is millions of guys who have great bodies and are good-looking," Mel stopped speaking for a while thinking how she could convey what she wanted to ask Tamara.

"I want to know how you would want your boyfriend to treat you. Catching up on what you said before I don't think you like to be cheated on or beaten." Tamara let out a deep sigh.

"Well obviously I like someone who would treat me like a queen. Will never hurt me intentionally and is attentive and cares about me. Someone I can rely on and would help me in times of need," Tamara said pouring the orange juice Mel had offered her earlier.

"Let me ask you a crucial question. Is Tyris like this person you have described? You are quite sensible because you are not asking too much. What you said is the basis for a healthy relationship," Mel gave Tamara time to answer but there was no reply. She looked like she was going to burst into tears again but Mel wasn't going to let her off easily.

"You can take your time and be honest," her voice was filled with sympathy.

"No he is not. He's nothing like that. He treats me like I'm nothing," Tamara finally admitted after a long pause.

"That settles it then. You are lucky that unhealthy relationship is over and don't try and reconcile your relationship with him but move on with your life. I'm sure you'll make it without him and you'll be happier. What is the point of going out with someone who makes you cry most of the time," Mel advised.

"But he loves me. I know he denied it today but he had always told me he does," Tamara said still trying to hold on to Tyris.

"Love is shown by actions not just words. You should be able to say that my man loves me because he does this and that not just because he says so. Let me get a bible and read you a verse which talks about what love is and you can judge if that applies to what you had with Tyris." When Mel said that Tamara was sceptical at first but agreed to hear the verse out of curiosity. She had never read a bible or been to church. Mel read her 1 Corinthians 13 which say "love is kind and patient, never jealous, boastful, proud or rude. Love isn't selfish or quick tempered. It doesn't keep a record of wrongs that others do. Love rejoices in the truth, but not in evil, love is always supportive, loyal, hopeful and trusting. Love never fails!" Tamara was impressed she never thought the bible talked about love like that. At that moment she was so fascinated she wanted to know more about what was in the bible. Mel offered her one of the bibles she had and Tamara accepted. Mel informed her that the book of Corinthians was full of information about relationships and it would be a good start. Tamara's face quickly lit up. Mel silently asked God to touch Tamara's heart when she reads the bible and give her a revelation of Himself and His love.

"Thanks Mel," Tamara said getting up to leave "You are truly an amazing person. I came here depressed but somehow you managed to lift my spirit. I don't feel suicidal anymore and somehow I am looking forward to discovering what life has in store for me. From now on I'm going to start hanging out with you. There is a positive vibe around you," Tamara complimented Mel.

"Thanks love but I just know that if it wasn't for God I wouldn't be the person I am right now. It is a pleasure to help someone. I believe I went through heart break and depression so that I could help others handle what I went through better."

"I am looking forward to reading about this God you always talk about and Mel thanks for showing me love even though I was such a bitch to you," Tamara apologised "I was jealous of you and envied you." Mel was taken by surprise; she never thought Tamara would be envious of any girl. She seemed like she had high self esteem and thought she was better than everyone else "why! Why would you be envious of me?" Mel asked curious.

"It is because you seem to have your life together. Even though you don't have a boyfriend you don't let that ruin your joy. You seem so happy whatever is going on around you. I know I tried to put you down loads of times but you never let it get to you," Tamara replied.

Mel studied her for a moment and said, "my joy comes from God, not a boyfriend, money or anything else. I don't see the reason why I should lose happiness because I don't have money or a boyfriend as if my happiness depends on that. As long as I know that God loves me and cares about my well being I will be happy."

"Are you telling me you don't care about having a boyfriend and you are always happy?" Tamara asked surprised.

"Believe me I would like to have a boyfriend. Everyday I pray to God that he will hook me up with a great guy. I am not going to settle for anyone which is the reason why I'm single but I have faith that in due time I will find that special person. All I need to do is do is wait patiently and not lose my faith. God says he will give us our heart desires so since I desire to be married to a great man of God and have children it will surely happen. To your other question, I am not always happy, sometimes I break down and cry or feel sad but knowing that it is not the end of the world and God can deal with whatever concerns me and will strengthen me to go on with my life and be happy."

"You are an interesting lady. I should leave now or else we will talk the whole night and be late for class tomorrow," Tamara said heading to the door still holding on to the bible. She lived in the same block of flats with Mel just a few floors away. When she had left Mel prayed that Tamara would give her life to God. Winning people over to God was important to Mel. She knew that God directed Christians to preach the gospel to non believers and win people into the kingdom.

Five

*T*he winter weather had turned unexpectedly mild and Mel was enjoying the unseasonably warm weather.

"Why are you hanging out with Tamara after the way she used to treat you and don't you know that bad company corrupts good character," Amanda told her bluntly as she sat with Mel in the university cafeteria eating lunch. She wasn't happy that her best friend was getting on too well with her arch enemy.

"I'm helping her get through a rough time and I think she needs all the love and support she can get. Day after day I am seeing a change in her. She has become quite devoted in studying the bible and things of God," Mel informed her friend.

"I know that bad company corrupts good character and the bible even says it but in this instance I am not trying to follow her lifestyle but trying to influence her positively. As Christians it is our duty to help those in need without discriminating on basis of bad character. In proverbs the bible says whenever you possibly can do well to those who need it. Never tell your neighbours to wait until tomorrow if you can help them now. If Jesus can forgive all the people who crucified him and all our sins then I have no right not forgiving someone else for I had needed and received forgiveness from God."

"What you said make sense. God told us to forgive those who offend or harm us." Amanda was quite a sensible lady and wasn't afraid to admit when she was wrong.

"Knowing Tamara though, watch out because she might turn against you later," Amanda added.

"Well I am not helping her because I want a reward from her or anyone else but God. It is my duty to help those who need my help without expecting anything in return from them. I don't put too much faith in people but in God because people let you down and they hurt you whether intentionally or unintentionally so I don't let people get to me when they do," Mel confessed.

"You're right I always breakdown when the people I love and trust hurt me." Amanda said.

"Another thing you can do in order to avoid breaking down when the people you love hurt you is putting God first in your life. When I was going out with my ex boyfriend I put him first before God. When he hurt me I thought life was over because instead of God being my everything I put him before God instead," Mel shared her story one more time.

Amanda said in a conciliatory tone "I'm sure if you had made God your everything you would have been able to move on better, knowing that your happiness comes from God not your boyfriend." Amanda glanced at her watch. It was almost time for the next lesson so the two ladies cleared after themselves and left. They were classmates so they went together to the class. Tamara was not in the same class with them, she studied law.

*A*fter some time Amanda and Tamara managed to sort things out between each other and became good friends. Mel was very happy to see her two friends getting along. Tamara gave her life to God after a few months of studying the bible when she started believing every word she read in the bible. Mel and Amanda were there to assist Tamara from the transition of being a non believer to a Christian. She had so much zeal for God that she started talking about God all the time. She managed to get over Tyris with much difficulty at first but after some time he was history to her. It also helped when she fell in love with an eligible bachelor at church. Daniel was medium height, unremarkable features, blond hair and an intelligent good-looking face. She was surprised that good guys like her boyfriend Daniel still existed. She had never been treated well by her previous boyfriends.

"I can't believe Daniel has never requested that we sleep together. I thought guys were only interested in sleeping with me. I don't deserve him," Tamara told Mel. She had been going out with Daniel for about five months.

Mel sighed. She smiled at her friend.

"That is what it is supposed to be. God forbids us sleeping with people who we are not married to. In Corinthians Paul writes that the body is not for sexual immorality but for the Lord ," Mel added.

Tamara felt a shiver go through her "I know that now. That is why I am saying I don't deserve a guy like Daniel because I used to sleep around," Tamara was worried.

"Don't even for a second believe that you don't deserve to be loved because of what you did in the past. When you gave your life to Jesus you became a new creation and God forgave all your sins and you should forgive yourself too. You are entitled to all the blessings that belong to those that love God and don't let anyone including yourself tell you otherwise despite your past. We have all fallen short of God's glory."

"Thank you love," Tamara said giving Mel a hug. "You always have helpful words when I need them."

"Well the bible encourages us not to use harmful words, but only helpful words, the kind that build up and provide what is needed, so that what you say will do good to those who hear you," Mel grinned.

"One thing that makes me very proud of you is that you don't seem jealous when other people prosper or are blessed by God. You seem to be genuinely rejoicing with me for finding a good man even though you haven't managed to find that special person yourself."

"I am clever enough to know that I have to rejoice when God blesses other people because I know that whatever he did to you he will be able to do it to me if I remain faithful to him, it is only a matter of time."

Six

*O*utside the sky exploded into icy sheets of rain. Mel thought the weather was also reflecting how she was feeling.

"I can't take it anymore," Mel sobbed. She had gone to say goodbye to her spiritual mother Mrs Robinson. Mrs Robinson was a tall natural brunette and had earned the reputation of been a gracious hostess. She was the pastor's wife at her church.

Mel had finished her degree and was now going back home to London.

"What is the matter?" Mrs Robinson asked worried. She knew that Mel would be very emotional when saying goodbye but she seemed more distraught than expected.

"I don't know if I will ever get married. At 25 years I thought I would be at least in a stable relationship probably engaged but I don't even know any prospective boyfriend. I'm beginning to think that there is something wrong with me," Mel said with tears running down her cheeks. The past few months people at university and church had been speculating about Mel's single status. Some people from church had been telling her that she might even be cursed just because she was not in a relationship although she was really beautiful. They couldn't believe a beautiful girl like

Mel was not engaged to be married. Some folks at her university had been poking fun at her; making remarks like "it is because you keep going on about God that makes you remain single." Previously Mel was not bothered by people's opinion but now she was beginning to believe them. She had been praying for a life partner but it seemed like God was not answering that prayer. She was beginning to think that God was punishing her for sleeping with Brandon a long time ago or it was because she was cursed. Mel told Mrs Robinson all her fears and what people had been saying about her. Mrs Robinson prayed before giving Mel advice.

"Do not lose faith now Mel. I have always admired your unwavering confidence in God. Don't start losing faith now. I believe you are not cursed because he who God blesses, no man can curse. In due time you will see results but all you can do is to keep praying and hold on to your faith. God says he knows our needs and we shouldn't worry about our life because if God can clothe the grass of the field, how much more will he clothe us who are more valuable than grass."

Mrs Robinson stopped speaking for a while and went to check on her two young children who were playing in the back garden. When she came back she continued with her discourse to Mel who was listening intensely.

"I know how it feels like praying for something but it seems like there is no answer to your prayer. All you have to do is be patient as God will bless you in his own time. You can't put a timescale on when you will receive the blessing, simply trust that God will bless you with your life partner when it is the right time. Know that you never have victory without conflict and when trouble comes it is a sure sign that you are about to get blessed. Delay is not denial; sometimes God allows your blessings to be delayed so that when it happens his glory will be known. All these people who have been afflicting you will bite their lips when God begins to bless you. Don't worry about anything just continue to seek God because in John chapter 15 Jesus said "if you abide in me, and my words abide in you, you will ask what you desire and it shall be done for you." Maybe God was waiting for you to finish your education and maybe your future husband is in London. You are beautiful inside out and I am positive you will find a great man who loves you it's only a matter of time. "

"Thanks for the uplifting words. I feel much better now." Mel said gratefully. She knew that if someone had come to her with her problem she would have told them to wait upon the Lord but for a moment she had lost hope that God would bless her. Tamara and Amanda were both engaged now and Mel just felt left out as if God has forsaken her.

"I will definitely come back to see you and the other people at church whenever I can make the time", Mel said as she gave Mrs Robinson a hug.

"I wish you all the best in life and just remember that Philippians says that God is able to supply all your needs according to his riches in glory by Jesus Christ. Paul in Philippians also wrote that we should not be anxious for anything but in everything by prayer and supplication with thanksgiving, make our requests known to God and the peace of God, which surpasses all understanding, will guard our hearts and minds through Christ Jesus," Mrs Robinson concluded.

Mel thought about the verses in Luke chapter 11 where Jesus talked about how a friend will help you not because you are a friend but because of being persistent. Jesus said "I say to you, though he will not rise and give him because he is his friend, yet because of his persistence he will rise and give him as many as he needs. So I say to you, ask, and it shall be given to you; seek and you will find; knock, and it will be opened to you." Mel decided that day that she would be persistent in seeking God and asking for a wonderful husband.

Seven

When they arrived at the party, the place was already crowded with guests. They were greeted at the entrance hall by a friendly waiter. They were escorted to the party area were Mel saw some familiar faces. The music had begun playing and people were dancing. The repertoire was mostly soul music. The guests were enjoying themselves tremendously. Those who were not dancing were helping themselves from the silver trays of drinks being offered or from the buffet tables set up along both sides of the room. The room looked spectacular and was filled with different coloured balloons floating in the ceiling and happy birthday banners.

"Who's that guy?" Mel asked her new friend Tadiwa. She was an attractive black woman, had a voluptuous body and short black hair. It was now five months since Mel returned to London. She was still single even though every other aspect of her life was flourishing. She had no trouble getting a well paid job at a GP's surgery twenty miles from her parents' house. She had loads of support from family and friends and had settled well at her workplace already finding favour with the manager.

"I don't know him," Tadiwa replied "you can find out from

the birthday girl." The two ladies were at a house party of one of the ladies at church who was turning twenty-three. The residence was a lovely house. It was quite charming and exceptionally spacious throughout. It had an entrance hall, cloakroom, five double bedrooms three with en-suite shower rooms, family bathroom, three reception rooms, kitchen/breakfast room, garden with patio area and double garage. They were both invited and made sure they attended as Samantha the birthday girl had told them she would be mad if they didn't come. Samantha was black-American, medium height, a bit plump and had a friendly pretty face.

"We wouldn't miss it for the world," they had both promised Samantha.

"Don't worry about it. I just thought he's a stranger to me," Mel explained but there was more to the story than that. Somehow she kept being drawn to that guy and for the first time in years Mel was attracted to a guy instantly. He was a tall, slim, athletic black man with beautiful brown eyes and a flawless complexion. He was wearing a white shirt and a soft grey suit jacket in stretch cotton satin and straight dark blue jeans and white trainers. He had broad shoulders and Mel could see his amazing smile from across the room. He seemed to be enjoying his conversation with a group of people.

"I'll be surprised if you are not eyeing him like most of the single ladies in the room. He is extremely good looking and I must say you two would make a great couple," Tadiwa was not deceived by Mel pretending not to be interested "if I was single I would be eyeing him too," Tadiwa chided.

"Well you can't just say I would make a good couple with someone just based on looks. We don't know anything about his character or if he loves God," Mel reasoned "how do I look though?" Mel was wearing an elegant, knee length satin cocktail dress which had spaghetti straps and a sweetheart neckline. The back had an unusual tie detail and the asymmetric skirt had a chiffon layer over the top and high slit at the leg.

"You look smashing and you're right looks are not enough but if he is single there is no harm in getting to know him and asking those who know him about his character", Tadiwa suggested.

"You are assuming he's interested in me and I will be surprised if he's single," Mel said still looking at the direction of the guy. For a second he looked at their direction and their eyes met. Mel quickly looked away, she was very embarrassed to be caught looking at him. It wasn't like her to do that. Within a minute Mel was startled to hear a deep male voice behind her saying "hello!" When Mel turned around she was startled to see it was that guy she had just been looking at.

"Hello," he said again and extended his hand to greet them. Tadiwa shook hands with him and Mel still shaken only managed to say a low "hello."

"My name is Michael", he introduced himself "what are your names?" he grinned baring beautiful white teeth. Mel was mesmerised, he was even better-looking close up and oozed confidence.

"I'm me-me- Mel," she stammered. Tadiwa started laughing lightly. She couldn't believe Mel was blushing. She had always seen Mel comfortable around men and this was a first.

"I'm Tadiwa," she said after composing herself in a serious tone.

"Nice to see you ladies. Are you enjoying the party?" Michael said.

"The party is great", Tamara answered after a pause. She thought Mel would reply but she seemed to be in her own world with the faraway look on her face. "So what brings you to the party?" Tamara asked Michael curiously.

"Samantha is my cousin. Our mothers are sisters," he replied. Samantha's mother was married to an American man and had just recently come back to live in Britain. Michael was thrilled because now she was seeing her cousins regularly instead of when he was holidaying in America. As soon as he finished speaking Samantha's brother came to drag him away. He wanted to introduce him to his girlfriend who had just arrived.

"See you later ladies," Michael managed to say as he was being dragged away.

"Bye," the two ladies said together grinning.

"Isn't he lovely? He's so friendly and charming," Tadiwa commented.

"He's ok," Mel replied trying to hide the effect Michael was having on her.

Tadiwa said fervently "he's the perfect guy for you and if I am not mistaken I saw a twinkle in his eyes when he was looking at you. I hope things will work out for both of you."

"Stop it", Mel said lazily "before you start planning our wedding. Consider the possibility that he might be married or not interested in me for all we know."

"I am just saying if he asks you out agree and get to know him rather than just dismissing him. You can ask Samantha about him. She won't lie to you if he is bad news," Tadiwa advised.

"Enough of that", Mel snapped "We are discussing as if the guy has asked me out. I don't think I will ever see him again."

"Why so negative. You are always the one preaching about being positive and saying positive words whatever the circumstance," Tamara said sardonically.

Mel nodded "I know but I just don't want to get ahead of myself. All I am going to say is if it is meant to be it will be."

She shrugged wanting very much to end the conversation. Mel proposed that they go back to her car and get the presents and go home shortly after the cake had been cut. Samantha's aunt had just announced that the cake will be cut in ten minutes. They didn't want to be late for church the next day so left the party early.

Eight

"*I* can't believe this," Mel whispered to Tadiwa.

What she couldn't believe was seeing Michael again. The chairman had introduced the person who was preaching that day as Mr Johnson a guest preacher. He was a bishop at a well known church in Hertfordshire. When he came on the pulpit, he introduced his family. Firstly he introduced his wife who was of medium built, probably in her early fifties, had a round face and warm dark brown eyes. She was dressed smartly in an expensive looking suit. It was made with summer light new wool, crafted with loving attention to detail. The suit was feminine and close fitting and the jacket had flap pockets, the skirt had dividing seams that open out to create a slightly flared effect at the hem. She was wearing grey high heeled shoes that matched her suit. The next person he called was his son Michael. When he came to stand next to his father, Mr Johnson said. "This is my youngest son out of four children. He is my only child who is still single until one lucky lady comes to whisk him away," people started laughing and they were a lot of happy single ladies in church including Mel. Mr Johnson said that before he began preaching he would like his son to sing first. Michael started playing the keyboard and singing there is none like Jesus. He was an extremely good singer and before he even finished people were clapping and joining in. when he finished singing his father praised him saying how he was a good son, loved God and was a great singer. Michael thanked his father for his praises and the church members for a warm welcome and went to sit down so that his father could get on with preaching. Mr Johnson preached a soul searching message and most people after the service commented on how his message had touched them. After church Mel couldn't believe it when she bumped into Michael when she was alone for a moment while Tadiwa went to the ladies.

"Hi Mel," he greeted her with a big smile.

"Hi," Mel replied more composed this time than the day before. Somehow his presence was not intimidating to her anymore. She felt very comfortable around him this time around.

"Nice to see you again. I was afraid I would never see you again until Samantha told me you go to the same church", Michael said to Mel's surprise.

There was a dazed expression on her face "Why would you even ask about me?"

"Because you seem like a lovely girl and I just want to know you better" he said looking at Mel and smiled "you look absolutely gorgeous". Mel was wearing a trouser suit which was flamboyant and straight out of the top drawer. It was beautifully decorated with French lace, a sophisticated contrast to the pinstripe pattern. Her trouser was wide-cut with broad contoured waistband and pressed creases.

Mel was watching him wide-eyed "thanks."

"You left the party early so we couldn't get better acquainted," he hesitated.

"Is it possible for you to give me your number?" Mel couldn't believe it. This guy was really asking for her number. She wanted to jump up and down screaming thank you God but she remained calm as she didn't want to look too eager. There was a pause.

"So are you going to give me your number Mel? I can even beg if you want," Michael asked again when Mel hadn't said anything.

"I'll give you her number," Tadiwa said startling Michael and Mel. She had overhead Michael asking for Mel's number without them noticing she was there.

"Oh, how are you Tadiwa?" Michael asked.

"You are very good with names. I can't believe you remembered my name," Tadiwa spoke her mind. She was quite outspoken, friendly and honest.

"It's a gift," Michael replied laughing "I would rather Mel give me her number herself though."

"Ok! I will leave you two to talk then," Tadiwa walked away. She pinched Mel a little bit before she left fearing she won't give him her number. After a while Mel gave him her number and he promised he would be in touch. He even introduced her to his father and told him she was his new friend and to expect to see more of Mel. That same day they spent some extra time getting acquainted as people enjoyed the buffet prepared for the fellowship meal after the church service. Michael told Mel that he worked as an executive accountant at a big accounts firm in central London. He was the youngest executive accountant having been promoted quickly because he was extremely good at his job. He also informed her he lived in North London on his own in a one bedroom apartment he bought two years earlier when he was only twenty-five years old. He kept saying thankfully that if it wasn't for God he wouldn't have achieved what he did at an early age. He said that the only thing that was missing in his life was a wife as he hadn't found that special person yet. He had ended things with his ex girlfriend two years ago when she dumped him because he was talking about God too much and involved in the church activities a lot. His ex-girlfriend was a Christian too but wasn't passionate about the things of God like Michael. Mel also told him about herself and their conversation was cut short when the caretaker started making arrangements to lock up the building. Mel couldn't believe how easy it was to talk to Michael. She talked to him as if she was speaking to an old friend rather than a stranger she had just met.

Nine

Over the following months, the dancing January winds had given way to spring and then summer, and winter clothes were replaced by light, cool outfits. Mel dressed carefully wondering if she was going to get good or bad news that day. She chose a classic black dress which was classic and feminine. It had a slightly plunging 'V' neck and shirred shoulders and a string you could tie in the back. Mel and Michael's relationship continued to blossom and the two of them shared a common interest in almost everything. Michael called Mel almost everyday and they talked for long hours most of the time. They talked about everything from their goals and dreams, what was happening in their lives and their ideal mates. They had become best friends and cared about each other a lot. It was now six months since they first met and Mel was nervous because she was meeting Michael that day to review their relationship. They were not officially boyfriend and girlfriend as they agreed that they would be platonic friends for a few months so that they get to know each other better and spent time together without the pressure of been involved romantically and if they both wanted to start dating they would. "I would want you to be my girlfriend right now," Michael had said five month ago "but I don't want to put pressure on you. From past experiences I think it's better if we get to know each other first for some time as just friends and if you think I am the right guy for you just as I think you are the right girl for me we will then start dating." Mel agreed as she reasoned that even though she wanted a deeper commitment from Michael it was better to know each other first and see if they both felt the same way after some time.

"What time did you say Michael was arriving?" Mrs Donovan asked Mel who was waiting for him with little patience in the dining room.

"Anytime from now," she said looking at her watch "he called me twenty minutes ago saying he was on his way. I'm so anxious to know if he wants this relationship to go to a deeper level."

"I'm sure he does," Mrs Donovan assured her daughter. She had grown fond of Michael. He seemed to have a positive impact on her daughter. He brought out the best in her and made her happy. Mrs Donovan had met him a couple of times when he had come to take Mel out and he was always polite, charming and very respectful. After a few minutes they heard the door bell. Mel sprang up from the couch and started straightening her clothes "how do I look?" she asked her mother anxiously.

"You look beautiful as usual honey and do I have to keep telling you that you are dressed to impress."

"Thanks Mum! I will go and answer the door. I'm sure it's Michael at the door."

"Can someone answer the door," Mr Donovan shouted from the TV room.

"Ok dad," Mel shouted back. Mrs Donovan went to join her husband who was watching television like he does at weekends. They both didn't work weekends and took that time to spend some quality time together.

"Hi!" Mel greeted Michael with a massive smile when she opened the door. He was dressed in casual wear.

"Hi!" he said handing Mel a bunch of flowers.

"Thanks," Mel said smiling shyly and giving him a hug.

"You are welcome," he said entering the house.

Mel showed him where his parents were and then joined them after she had put her flowers in a vase.

"How is Bishop?" Mr Donovan asked Michael when they had finished greeting each other.

"He is fine. I was with him and mum yesterday." After some time Mel excused herself going in the kitchen to prepare some lunch. When she left Michael got the opportunity to talk to Mel's parents about his intentions.

"I and your daughter have been friends for quite some time now and I care about her a lot," Michael said nervously. Mr Donovan intimidated him a little bit but he knew he had no choice but to be courageous and say what he wanted to.

"I want to know if it is ok with you if I was to marry your daughter. Will I have your blessing?"

"What!" Mr Donovan exclaimed "I didn't know you two are dating. I thought you were just friends."

"Don't be naïve honey. I knew even though they were not officially dating the children are in love. If Michael didn't love Mel he wouldn't put so much effort in building a relationship with her," Mrs Donovan reasoned.

He leaned back in his chair "If you want to marry my daughter you have my blessing and knowing how my wife thinks highly of you she will be happy if you marry our daughter."

"He's right. If you marry my daughter I feel she will be in the right hands and I want to praise you for asking our permission first. Most young men don't do that these days. I hear of people getting married without their parents' knowledge or support."

"My father always told me that before I get involved with any girl I should have the parents' support," Michael said happily. He was happy Mel's parents had accepted him as their future son in law.

"I just want to let you know though that whatever you do never hurt my daughter. I want you to love her like she deserves or you'll have to deal with me." There was seriousness in his voice. He was very protective of his daughter and didn't want to see her hurt again. Michael felt a shiver go through him. He didn't know Mr Donovan could be very tough.

He said earnestly "I love your daughter and I will never do anything to hurt her. Not intentionally of course."

"It's good you came to us but it is up to Mel to decide if she wants to marry you. She's old enough to make that decision," Mrs Donovan added.

Michael said cautiously "ok! If you don't mind can we please keep this among ourselves and I will propose to Mel when we go out later today." Mel entered the room again before her parents could answer. She looked at Michael and felt a warm glow. I love this guy, she thought. She announced that lunch was ready and requested that everyone go to the dining room. They did as they were told and enjoyed the Shepard's pie Mel had made. After lunch Michael insisted on helping Mel do the dishes. He proposed that they go to the town centre to watch a movie and eat dinner later at a restaurant. Mel agreed.

As they drove away in Michael's car, Mel studied him as he drove, she noted that he was a skilful driver. They watched an action romantic movie and later went to have dinner over candlelight. They dined at a sophisticated Italian restaurant which served authentic food using fresh seasonal produce. They finished eating without any discussion of their relationship and Mel thought it was because he wanted to remain just friends. Her thoughts were interrupted when Michael took her hand in his and said "Mel you are my best friend and I love you so much." Her heart jumped with excitement. It was the first time Michael had said I love you to her.

"I think you are the right lady for me because we get along well, we share the same values and care about each other a lot. My parents love you and approve of our friendship. Speaking to people who know you affirmed my knowledge that you are truly a godly, loving and friendly person." He added looking lovingly in Mel's eyes.

She was beaming "I think you might be exaggerating the comments." She tried to be modest. She felt a surge of excitement when Michael said "what I am trying to say to you is — will you marry me? I want to get old with you, love you always, protect and provide for you." He took out three small boxes which each contained a diamond ring and placed them on the table. Mel was shocked, she had no idea Michael wanted to marry her but never the less she was thrilled. God has answered my prayers, she thought. Michael was her dream guy. He was funny, honest, caring, very attentive, good-looking, gentle, passionate about helping people in need and a devoted Christian.

He smiled reassuringly "what do you say Mel? I know we haven't dated but I don't just want to be your boyfriend but your fiancé. I want to marry you". He said kneeling down "will you?"

Mel smiled and said without hesitating "of course I will". She had known for a long time that Michael was the man she wanted to marry. The people around them who had overhead the proposal started cheering and some came over to congratulate them. He patted her hand, "now young lady there are the rings before you and if you don't mind, choose which one you want as your engagement ring." All the rings were so beautiful she didn't know which one to choose. Finally she chose the one she was drawn to the most. It was a three stoned diamond ring set in platinum.

Ten

Michael was furious, in fact he was more than furious. He was like a raging animal. He had just been told that Mel was cheating on him.

"Are you hundred percent sure?" he had asked with a frown on his face.

"Would I lie to you? Of course it's true. I saw her kissing another guy and I am definite it was Mel". Michael had found it hard to believe Mel would cheat on him especially when they were due to get married in three months time. They had been engaged for six months now and their relationship was getting stronger and stronger. Is Mel really capable of cheating, Michael thought as he drove to Mel's house coming from Samantha's house. They had planned to meet that day and go shopping together but Michael was not in the mood anymore. He decided that he would just go and see Mel so that he could confront her despite Samantha's request that he shouldn't say anything and just find another excuse to break up with her. Maybe Samantha was lying, he thought but quickly dismissed the idea by telling himself that Samantha had no reason to lie and knowing her he didn't think she was capable of telling a lie which could destroy people's lives. He was still battling with his thoughts when he arrived at Mel's house. Mel welcomed him cheerfully as usual just to be surprised by his cold response. "What's the matter honey?" she asked with a concerned look on her face. She thought maybe something bad had happened to his family or work.

"We need to talk," his voice was full of sorrow.

"Need to talk!" she exclaimed

Michael is acting very weird, she thought. She had never seen him like this before. He looked very angry and was not as loving to her like he used to be.

"Are you going to come in?" Mel asked when Michael remained standing outside.

"No thanks", he answered tonelessly.

"Ok! Let me quickly grab my handbag and sunglasses then we will be on our way." It was summer time and it was scotching hot outside. After a few minutes they were on their way to the lakeside. Michael told Mel he didn't feel like going shopping anymore and she agreed to go for a barbecue at the lakeside instead. When they were parked Michael told Mel what he had heard whilst still sitting in the car.

"You are joking right?" Mel laughed. She didn't think Michael would actually believe she was capable of cheating.

Michael said in a serious tone. "What's so funny about you cheating on me?" That is when Mel realised he was dead serious.

"How can you just believe what you hear from people about me without giving me the benefit of the doubt?" she stopped for a moment and took a deep sigh. "Have I ever given you any reason to believe I am cheating?"

"I don't know Mel. I am not with you twenty four hours a day," he answered angrily.

"I am not with you twenty four hours a day too but I don't

think you are cheating. It is all about trust Michael". Mel was beginning to be angry too. She was disappointed that Michael would accuse her for cheating based on what he heard from someone.

"Did you cheat or not?" he asked.

"For your own information I never cheated on you and I will never cheat on anyone. It is just not my style," she said furiously "I'm upset that you don't trust me. Trust is one of the most important ingredients of a good marriage. You can't just believe what people tell you about me without investigating if this could be true for yourself. If you really knew me you would know that I love you so much and I would never even look at another man twice."

"Don't act like you are the victim here,", Michael ignored what Mel had just said "You are the one who cheated on me despite showing you love and treating you very well. I gave you everything you wanted."

"Michael stop," she demanded.

Michael ignored her. "Why, why Mel?" he asked "Is it because we are not sleeping together?"

"You know and I have told you all the time that I believe in sex after marriage like the bible instructs."

"You are not exactly a virgin are you? So it is clear you have slept with a guy before you were married."

"How could you say that Michael," she said in a raised voice "we discussed it before and you said you were fine with the fact that I was not a virgin. You assured me that my past was not going to be an issue and you were not going to judge me for a mistake I made when I was young and naïve. I didn't have the kind of relationship I have with God right now back then. It's not like you are a virgin yourself." Michael had told Mel before that when he was a teenager he went on a defiant phase and he slept with a girl just to get at his parents. "My parents were very strict and made sure we didn't do anything that was not in accordance with the word of God. At seventeen I thought I was all grown up and decided to sleep with a girl and told my parents what I had done so that they would know I was a man now," he had said.

One thing Mel loved about their relationship was that they were honest about everything. They were honest about how they felt, their past and when they were upset with one another. Michael was very open about everything it was refreshing. They talked about everything and when they had an argument they argued fairly without name calling or threatening each other but worked very hard to find solutions to their problems which was not very hard as both of them were willing to compromise if they were doing anything to make each other unhappy. This argument is much more serious and destructive than any other argument we've had, Mel thought sadly.

"I said your past didn't matter because I thought you were a different person but now that you've cheated on me, you have changed my perspective of you."

"What makes you sure that I cheated? Who told you?" Mel asked quietly fighting back the tears. She was beginning to think that their wonderful relationship was about to fall apart and her dream marriage shattered.

"I have been sworn to secrecy. Can't tell you but just know that it was from a reliable source. If it was just a random person I would have never believed it."

"Your source is not as reliable as you think because I am the one who really knows the truth and I am telling you I have never kissed anyone whilst going out with you," she said.

"I think I deserve to know who is trying to ruin our relationship after all we've been through together." Michael contemplated what she had just said for a minute then said "It was Samantha." Mel was shocked. How can Samantha make up such a lie? She thought Samantha liked her like she always said and was happy she was marrying her cousin. No wonder Michael believed I cheated but I am his fiancé. He should take my word and trust me if we are to get married, She thought.

She said out loud. "So what have you decided to do about all this since you are adamant that I cheated on you?"

"Right now I don't think I would want to marry someone who has cheated on me."

Mel was dumbfounded. "What exactly do you mean?" she said "Are you saying you want to cancel the wedding?"

"I don't want to decide anything hastily that I might regret so just give me time to think everything through and I will let you know after some time what I have decided."

Mel said "Whatever you decide just know that I don't want to marry someone who doesn't trust me and listens to gossip. So unless you decide that you trust me maybe we should just break up."

"Let's end this conversation until we have both cooled off because we might say things that we might regret later," he suggested.

Michael offered that they get out of the car and go for the barbecue but Mel refused. She didn't feel like eating anything at the moment and just wanted to go home. Michael agreed to take her home immediately.

Eleven

Mel was awakened by the sound of her parents speaking loudly. She laid still, her eyes tightly closed, thinking: I might have lost Michael for ever, God how can this be when I had high hopes for us. It had been five days since Michael confronted her about cheating and she had not heard from him since then. She tried to call him a couple of times but he ignored her calls and didn't return them. After a while she opened her eyes and started staring at the ceiling. Finally, reluctantly she forced herself to get out of bed. She was due to start work in a few hours time but her body ached. The past few days she had been working overtime trying to cope with what was happening with her and Michael. Mel thought she had come to terms with it, but suddenly the idea that they might break up suddenly assumed a reality that was immediate and terrifying. Everything within Mel screamed to deny what had happened with Michael but every time he didn't call the reality kept hitting her in fresh waves of shock. She went to have a shower and dressed slowly. She waited until her parents had gone and went down stairs to have some breakfast. She couldn't face her parents right now knowing she hadn't told them what was happening with her relationship and was avoiding them. She was hoping they will reconcile quickly before people knew about their tiff but with every day they didn't reconcile it was getting more and more difficult to keep quiet. She hadn't even told her best friend Tadiwa but knew she would have to tell her as soon as possible as she desperately needed to talk to someone. They had planned a month ago that all the bridesmaids should meet at Mel's house that weekend to discuss the role they were going to play in Mel's wedding and finalise issues about which dresses they were going to wear. Her bridesmaids were going to be Amanda, Tadiwa, Tamara and Mel's cousin Tanya. They had decided that Mel will choose the bridesmaids and Michael the grooms' men which consisted of his best friend Edward and three of his cousins. Mel thought about telling all the bridesmaids not to come but decided against it as it was a long time since she saw most of them and knew the reunion would be a good thing. If I tell people not to come it means that I am saying that I believe the wedding is off and the relationship is over and the word of God teaches that whatever you believe and say with your mouth will come to pass, Mel thought as she sat down on the breakfast table.

She started recalling the message that her pastor had preached a few weeks ago. He had said the words we speak are life and death, she had heard this message a couple of times before but had never really taken it seriously neither had she been careful to make sure she spoke positive words over her life or other people. The pastor made it clear that there was power in what we said with our mouth. He said whatever you say can come to life for example if you keep saying I am unworthy, broke and I am not going to achieve anything in life this will come to pass eventually, but if you keep saying you are rich and you are a great person of God, even though it might not be a reality in your life at the moment it will happen because you keep confessing it and putting actions to your words. He said never to let go of your desire and that you have to keep saying it for it to manifest. He also said the devil works by making you believe lies, when you speak those lies the negative things can affect you and cause you to fear. The problem is faith doesn't go together with fear and God needs your faith in order to work in your life. He says if you believe and confess with your mouth you can move mountains and that applies if you confess the negative things too. He gave examples to illustrate his point. Like if you have pain in your chest and maybe your family has a history of heart attacks and you start saying oh my, I am going to have a heart attack. This is opening a door to the devil to bring to pass evil in your life. The pastor stated that the thing to do is that even though you have chest pain don't be afraid, but start confessing Scriptures that say 'I am healed' and don't let your faith waver whatever circumstance you are in and don't say things like I can't make it.

Mel made a vow that from that point she would only speak positive things. She declared that she was going to marry Michael no matter what. She decided not to look at the circumstances but believe that God will make a way where there seemed to be no way and they will get married as planned. She didn't know exactly how things were going to work out but knew from past experiences that if you cast your burdens to Jesus he will help you out.

Twelve

Mel arranged for her family to leave the house to her and the bridesmaids so that they wouldn't have any distractions. Her parents took that time to go out and enjoy a romantic lunch and go to the theatre in the evening. Mel had bought them theatre tickets so that they could go and see their favourite stand up comedian. The visitors all arrived at close intervals and Mel gave them all a warm welcome. Tanya and Amanda both had beautiful baby girls now and Mel took turns to play with both babies. She loved children and couldn't wait to have her own children. Tanya advised that they get down to business and then catch up later. They all agreed on one dress and the ladies offered to pay for their own dresses. After a while Mel told them what was going on with Michael when they kept asking about him.

"That girl needs a beating;" Tamara yelled "how could she make up something like that, and Mel I can't believe you let her get away with it." Mel had not confronted Samantha and she tried to ring her once but there was no answer.

"You know I could never beat anyone. "Tamara said.

"I just said 'beating' as a figure of speech meaning telling her off."

"She's right Mel. I know you are all about forgiving and being loving to your enemies but there is no harm in confronting Samantha and finding out why she lied if she really did. Michael could have lied."

"No way" Mel interjected "Michael would never lie about something like that especially if it means implicating an innocent person." She trusted and knew Michael enough to know it was not like him to lie and she had witnessed the hurt in his eyes. This was not an excuse to break up with her like Tadiwa was implying.

Tanya handed Mel her phone. "Here's my mobile call that lady and find out her side of the story. She might answer if you call with a different number. You can't just let her off easily. Tell her what she did was totally out of order."

Mel called Samantha with little persuasion as she was a firm believer in confronting people if they had hurt you or you didn't like something they had done. She could do this and then move on without having a grudge whether or not the person said they were sorry or changed their behaviour. Samantha answered her mobile phone and Mel asked her if she told Michael she was cheating. Samantha said she wasn't going to answer. Mel took it as a yes and said. "I don't know if you had mistaken me for someone else or you made it up but just know that I love Michael and your lie has hurt us. I hope you'll find it in you heart to tell Michael the truth." She hung up when she finished speaking.

"Everyone listen up," Amanda requested "There is no point in us dicing Samantha and depending on her to tell the truth. All we can do is turn to Jesus as he is our helper and source if we have got problems. What we are going to do is praise and worship God because if you take time to worship God he will deliver you in whatever situation you are in. We are going to sing praises to God as it is written in Psalm 100 that we should enter his gates with thanksgiving and into his courts with praise. We are going to join hands in prayer as

God says whenever two or more agree about anything on earth in my name it will be done. So we are going to agree that this wedding will happen and Mel will have a wonderful marriage". They sang Days of Elijah and two more songs and Tadiwa prayed saying; "God we thank you for whom you are, we magnify your name for you are holy and worthy. We are coming together in agreement that Michael will open his heart and love Mel unconditionally. I pray that whatever is hidden will come to light and the peace of God protect Mel's mind and heart through troubled waters. I declare that no weapon formed against her shall prosper". When Tadiwa finished praying the ladies continued to share the word of God and discuss their love lives. Mel prepared dinner for all her guests and they waited for her parents so that they could eat together. They all left after dinner except Tanya who was going to drive back home early Sunday morning. Mel was very happy to spend some time with her friends as they didn't normally see enough of themselves and only stayed in contact by phone.

Thirteen

*A*fter a few days Mel got a call from Michael. She had been waiting patiently for his call and was glad when he finally called. "Can we meet at the town centre?" Michael requested. Normally he would come and pick her at home but Mel thought no worries as it was better than nothing. She dressed carefully but casually not knowing what to expect. When they met Mel was shocked by the way he looked. He was rugged looking, dressed in old jeans, T- shirt and trainers and he looked scruffy and unshaven. There were bags around his eyes as if he hadn't slept for days. Mel had never seen him in this state before. He was always clean shaven and smart all the time. Mel's heart went out to him, he looked very disturbed.

"Do you want to eat something?" he asked quietly after greeting each other.

"I've just had lunch at home so I am fine. What about you?"

"I'm fine," he shrugged.

"Let's go and have a cup of coffee so that we can at least sit down and talk." Michael agreed and they went to the nearest coffee shop and ordered coffee and cookies. Michael didn't waste time and started saying "Mel I am sorry for not believing you. I know deep down in my heart now that you didn't cheat on me and even if you did it doesn't matter. I love you and missed you all the days I didn't see you. I don't want to lose you because you are the best thing that has ever happened to me." Mel was touched by his words. She felt exactly the same way and therefore could feel his pain.

"I love you Michael", she said "does it mean we are back together?"

"Did we ever break up?" he asked.

"I thought we had broken up because you didn't call me for almost two weeks and you were not taking my calls".

"It was just pride love. I didn't want to admit that I still wanted to marry you even when I thought you had cheated and I didn't want to seem weak to my cousins who were saying I shouldn't marry someone who had cheated on me."

"So why the change of heart?" she asked.

"Because I realised if I am going to have a good relationship with you I shouldn't believe other people above you or allow them to interfere in our marriage. I know now that I mustn't be swayed by people's opinions if they are negative. I promise to love you unconditionally and if I have a disagreement with you I will work things out with you instead of going to people who might not have good intentions towards us."

"Does it mean the wedding is on?" She asked dully.

"Of course. I can't wait to marry you and move in our house and have our two children." They had bought a house a couple of months ago and had discussed that they would want to start a family as soon as they got married. Michael was going to pay off the rest of the mortgage when he sold his apartment which had appreciated considerably.

"All we have to do is stay committed to our marriage whatever trials come our way. I'm sure we are going to have difficulties in our marriage but it is up to us to continue loving each other and not give up whenever a problem arises."

"That's true my love", he said "I would be silly to let go of a woman like you. I would say you are like that virtuous woman from the bible and a gift from God." Mel was thrilled to know that Michael thought much of her. She always strived to be a virtuous woman. She rehearsed the bible chapter which she knew clearly; "who can find a virtuous wife? For her worth is far above rubies. The heart of her husband safely trusts her so he will have no lack of gain. She does him good and not evil all the days of her life. She extends her hand to the poor and she reaches out her hand to the needy. She opens her mouth with wisdom and on her tongue is the law of kindness."

Michael said "I love the ending of the chapter which says charm is deceitful and beauty is passing, but a woman who fears the Lord, she shall be praised." When they finished their coffees they left the café hand in hand. They started walking around the shops window shopping laughing and discussing details about the wedding joyfully. It was as if they had never argued. They were both startled to see Samantha. She was coming out of a shoe shop they were passing.

Samantha said uncomfortably "oh, hallo guys." She looked startled to see them together.

Michael said smiling "hi cuz. What are you doing shopping during the week"? He teased.

"Just wanted to buy some shoes for work tomorrow and don't ask."

"How are you keeping girl?" Mel asked trying to break the ice in the frosty atmosphere between her and Samantha who was clearly not thrilled to see her.

"I'm fine," she replied still avoiding looking Mel in the eye.

"I'm fine too," Mel said watching Samantha closely.

"I'm surprised to see you two together and Michael you look terrible," Samantha said dryly.

"Did you think I would stay mad at my future wife for ever? I love her and nothing will tear us apart," Michael chided. Samantha was lost for words for a minute and she quickly recovered and said "I have a confession to make."

"Go ahead, " Michael prompted.

"I lied that I saw Mel cheating."

"Are you crazy?" Michael shouted. "How could you do something like that? I could have lost the love of my life." Michael was angry. He seemed even more furious than when he thought Mel was cheating.

"Calm down darling?" Mel said "At least give Samantha the chance to explain why she lied."

"Ok go on. Why?" Michael yelled.

Samantha said quietly embarrassed "Because I was mad you didn't ask me to be one of your bridesmaids."

"Don't you think you are too old to be getting petty because you are not going to be a bridesmaid," he commented.

Mel ignored Michael's comment and said "Sorry but I didn't know you felt that way. You should have told Michael or me that you wanted to be a bridesmaid and we could have worked something out."

"Don't apologise to her," Michael remarked angrily. "Samantha is the one who should be saying sorry to us and you being a bridesmaid is out of the question now. Bridesmaids should be people who have good intentions towards the bride."

"I'm sorry guys," she apologised. "I have been feeling guilty ever since and Mel I just want to say you are a good girl and my cousin is lucky to have you. I could never ask to be in your wedding after what I did."

"You can still participate at the wedding if you wish. I and Michael were discussing about having someone sing at our wedding when we enter the church and the reception. Since you are a very good singer you could sing for us then we don't have to hire a professional. We might even pay you as well." she paused and asked "Is it ok Michael if she sings at the wedding."

He contemplated for a moment and said "I guess she can if she wants."

"Would you be able to do it Samantha?" Mel asked.

"I will definitely be happy to do it," she answered smiling "I will do it for free as well. I would never accept money from you and singing is even better than been a bridesmaid to me." Samantha enjoyed singing and always took the opportunity gladly to sing at church or parties.

"Thanks for agreeing and we will organise for you to meet with the band for rehearsals. You've got less than two months to practice."

Samantha said enthusiastically "I'll definitely practice everyday." Singing at the wedding will definitely put me on the spotlight, Samantha thought happily.

"Which songs would you want me to sing?"

"We were thinking about 'loving you' and 'a moment like this.'" Mel answered.

"These are good songs and the good thing is I already know the words of the songs." She started singing:

"Loving you is easy cause you're beautiful

Loving you is more than just a dream come true

And everything that I do is out of loving you

La la la la la la la... do do do do do

No one else can make me feel

The colours that you bring

Stay with me while we grow old"

"That's very good," Michael interrupted.

"You sang it beautifully," Mel added.

"The words are just beautiful," Samantha said. "I think it is one of the greatest songs ever written. I better be going guys. We've been standing on the same spot for a long time people are beginning to wonder why."

Michael said "Bye. Send my love to your family."

Mel said "Take care and thanks again. We should stay in touch."

"For sure," Samantha said and left.

When she had gone Michael said "You have a big heart Mel. What you have just done with Samantha was unbelievable. I was ready to bite her head off but you were understanding and forgave her easily. You make me a better person Mel. You keep me in check."

"You've got a big heart too and it was understandable for you to be upset. I guess everyone gets angry but it is not good to stay angry at someone for a long period of time."

"I have obtained favour from God," Michael said.

"Why did you say that?" Mel asked surprised by Michael going off the current topic.

"Because Proverbs says "He who finds a wife finds a good thing, and obtains favour from God. My father told me that this doesn't apply to every woman and I am glad I found someone who is wife material— you."

"I love you. I promise to be good to you as long as I live," said Michael. Mel looked deeply into his eyes and said "I Love you too."

****